Adapted by Devin Cameron
Illustrated by Caroline Egan
Designed by Deborah Boone

 A Golden Book • New York

Copyright © 2004 Disney Enterprises, Inc.
All rights reserved under International and Pan-American Copyright Conventions. Published in the United States
by Golden Books, an imprint of Random House Children's Books, a division of Random House, Inc., New York,
and simultaneously in Canada by Random House of Canada Limited, Toronto, in conjunction with Disney Enterprises, Inc.
Golden Books, A Golden Book, A Little Golden Book, the G colophon,
and the distinctive gold spine are registered trademarks of Random House, Inc.
Library of Congress Control Number: 2003110451
ISBN: 0-7364-2214-5
www.goldenbooks.com
www.randomhouse.com/kids/disney
Printed in the United States of America

10 9 8 7 6 5 4 3 2 1

If you lived on a farm, what would you be?

A grumpy goat?

A playful piggie?

Or maybe you'd like to be a noisy rooster . . .

"Cock-a-doodle-doo!"

"cheep!"

"cheep!"

"cheep!"

. . . or a cheeping chick.

Or how about a big dairy cow?

Pearl had all of these animals
on her farm. They were her family.

But Pearl's farm was in **trouble**. Her cows, Grace, Maggie, and Mrs. Caloway, decided to get help. They would do anything for Pearl.

They left the farm and walked all the way
to . . . **TOWN!**

The cows were scared of town. "Look! There are no fences!" said Grace. "What keeps the people from roaming?"

There were strange noises
and people everywhere.

Soon the cows saw a familiar face.
It was Buck, the sheriff's horse.
    He told the cows that they needed
money to save Pearl's farm.

How could three dairy cows get
enough money to save a farm?
There was **one way**. . . .

Alameda Slim stole cows. He did it by
yodeling. The cows found the music so
sweet, they would follow him anywhere.

"YOOOO-de-lay-hee-hoooo!"

Now there was a reward out for Slim.
Anyone who captured him would receive
seven hundred and fifty dollars!

That was the exact amount Maggie, Mrs. Caloway,
and Grace needed to save their farm!

Rico, the bounty hunter, wanted to capture
Slim so he could get the reward. Buck wanted to
help Rico so he could become a hero.

Together they rode off to find Alameda Slim.

The cows wanted to capture Alameda Slim first.
Together they left to find the outlaw.

But Slim almost cow-napped the cows! Grace was the only cow who wouldn't follow him. Slim's yodeling didn't affect her. Grace saved her friends.

Maggie, Grace, and Mrs. Caloway would
not give up their search for Alameda Slim.
They decided to follow Slim's tracks.

They searched **HIGH** . . .

. . . and **LOW**.

They searched **WET** places . . .

. . . and **DRY** places.

At last they found Slim!

But how could three
dairy cows catch an outlaw?

Slim caught the cows instead!

Then Buck found out that his hero, Rico, was Slim's secret partner! Rico was really a bad guy. Buck realized he had been wrong about Rico and the cows.

Buck figured it was time to help the **real heroes**, Maggie, Grace, and Mrs. Caloway! So Buck bucked . . .

. . . and the cows **kicked!**

Buck helped the cows. Then he sent them on their way . . . to save the farm!
"Good luck!" he shouted.

The cows put Slim away
for good. They had had
enough adventure for one
week. It was time to settle
back **home on the range**.

And now Maggie, Grace, and Mrs. Caloway weren't just dairy cows. They were . . . **hero cows!**